Too Cut! Baby Sloths

by Rachael Barnes

Blastoff! Beginners

BELLWETHER MEDIA
MINNEAPOLIS, MN

Blastoff! Beginners are developed by literacy experts and educators to meet the needs of early readers. These engaging informational texts support young children as they begin reading about their world. Through simple language and high frequency words paired with crisp, colorful photos, Blastoff! Beginners launch young readers into the universe of independent reading.

Sight Words in This Book

a	eat	look	their
and	from	many	them
are	get	on	they
at	help	ride	to
come	in	so	
day	it	the	

This edition first published in 2023 by Bellwether Media, Inc.

No part of this publication may be reproduced in whole or in part without written permission of the publisher. For information regarding permission, write to Bellwether Media, Inc., Attention: Permissions Department, 6012 Blue Circle Drive, Minnetonka, MN 55343.

Library of Congress Cataloging-in-Publication Data

Names: Barnes, Rachael, author.
Title: Baby sloths / by Rachael Barnes.
Description: Minneapolis, MN : Bellwether Media, 2023. | Series: Blastoff! beginners: Too cute! | Includes bibliographical references and index. | Audience: Ages 4-7 | Audience: Grades K-1
Identifiers: LCCN 2022012971 (print) | LCCN 2022012972 (ebook) | ISBN 9781644876725 (library binding) | ISBN 9781648347184 (ebook)
Subjects: LCSH: Sloths--Infancy--Juvenile literature.
Classification: LCC QL737.E2 B37 2023 (print) | LCC QL737.E2 (ebook) | DDC 599.3/13--dc23/eng/20220322
LC record available at https://lccn.loc.gov/2022012971
LC ebook record available at https://lccn.loc.gov/2022012972

Text copyright © 2023 by Bellwether Media, Inc. BLASTOFF! BEGINNERS and associated logos are trademarks and/or registered trademarks of Bellwether Media, Inc.

Editor: Christina Leaf   Designer: Jeffrey Kollock

Printed in the United States of America, North Mankato, MN.

Table of Contents

A Baby Sloth!	4
Life with Mom	6
Growing Up!	18
Baby Sloth Facts	22
Glossary	23
To Learn More	24
Index	24

A Baby Sloth!

Look at the **newborn** sloth!
Hello, baby!

newborn sloth

Life with Mom

Baby sloths live in tall trees.

They ride on mom.
They hold on to her tummy!

Sometimes babies fall. Mom comes to get them.

Baby sloths rest during the day. They take many naps.

napping

Baby sloths drink milk from mom. They **nurse** a lot.

nursing

They learn to eat leaves and flowers.

Growing Up!

Baby sloths grow **coarse** hair.
It turns green.
It helps them hide.

coarse hair

They climb
on their own.
They are so slow!

climbing

Baby Sloth Facts

Sloth Life Stages

newborn   baby   adult

A Day in the Life

ride on mom

eat leaves and flowers

climb

Glossary

coarse — wiry and uneven

newborn — just born

nurse — to drink mom's milk

23

To Learn More

ON THE WEB

FACTSURFER

Factsurfer.com gives you a safe, fun way to find more information.

1. Go to www.factsurfer.com.

2. Enter "baby sloths" into the search box and click 🔍.

3. Select your book cover to see a list of related content.

Index

climb, 20, 21
day, 12
drink, 14
eat, 16
fall, 10
flowers, 16
green, 18
hair, 18
helps, 18

hide, 18
hold, 8
learn, 16
leaves, 16, 17
milk, 14
mom, 8, 10, 14
naps, 12, 13
newborn, 4, 5
nurse, 14, 15

rest, 12
ride, 8
slow, 20
trees, 6
tummy, 8

The images in this book are reproduced through the courtesy of: Eric Isselee, front cover, pp. 3, 4; Mark_Kostich, p. 5; Suzi Eszterhas/ SuperStock, pp. 6-7, 22 (newborn); Nature Picture Library/ SuperStock, pp. 8-9; Kristel Segeren, pp. 10 11, 18, 22 (climb); Víctor Santamaría González/ Alamy, pp. 12-13; belizar, pp. 14-15; Dean Bouton, pp. 16-17; Petr Simon, pp. 18-19; kungverylucky, pp. 20-21; Guillermo Ossa, p. 22 (baby); Akkharat Jarusilawong, p. 22 (adult); Manamana, p. 22 (ride); Damsea, p. 22 (eat); Suzy Molard, p. 23 (coarse); Charlie J Ercilla/ Alamy, p. 23 (newborn); ZUMA Press Inc/ Alamy, p. 23 (nurse).